BLEAK MIDWINTER

CHARLOTTE O'FARRELL

VELOX BOOKS

Published by arrangement with the author.

Copyright © 2024 by Charolotte O'Farrell.

All rights reserved.

No part of this publication may be reproduced, distributed, or transmitted in any form or by any means, including photocopying, recording, or other electronic or mechanical methods, without the prior written permission of the publisher, except as permitted by U.S. copyright law.

The story, all names, characters, and incidents portrayed in this production are fictitious. No identification with actual persons (living or deceased), places, buildings, and products is intended or should be inferred.

YOU'RE READING ANOTHER TERRIFYING COLLECTION FROM

VELOX BOOKS

FOLLOW VELOX TO KEEP THE NIGHTMARES COMING:

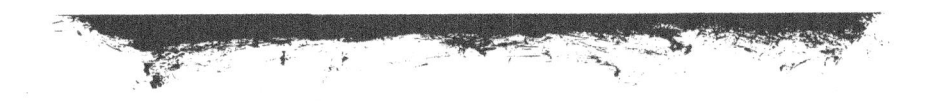

For R. & J., the two lights of my life—with lots of love.

Contents

Bleak Midwinter	1
Flashing Plastic Lights	23
Midnight Mass	29
Mistletoe-Ho-Ho	31
Snow on Snow	39
The Tinsel Murders	43
In Santa's Grotto	49
The Winter Plague	53
Haunted by Christmas Past	57
About the Author	61

Bleak Midwinter

I: CHRISTMAS EVE LOCK-IN

As soon as the nights start getting darker and summer starts to wane, I know The Question is coming.

It's happened at every workplace, every social gathering, every group I've ever been a part of. If I'm lucky, I make it to October without someone asking me The Question. But I've never made it beyond that. Sooner or later, someone always asks: "So, Sue, why don't you celebrate Christmas?"

And everyone who hears looks at me like I've just grown a second head.

Usually I mumble something about just not enjoying it. They normally leave me alone if I say it's against my religion (although, having been raised in a lukewarm weddings-and-funerals-only form of the Church of England, celebrating the birth of Jesus is not exactly a problem on that front). On the rare occasions I'm feeling particularly honest, I say I had a tragic experience around that time that I don't want to be reminded of. No-one but the rudest pries after that. They assume I lost a parent around then or something, probably.

I try to keep the weirder aspects of my hatred for Christmas under wraps. I don't tell them that the sound of rustling tinsel has sent me into a panic attack before. Or that seeing cartoony pictures of Santa's workshop—my gosh, all those creepy grinning *elves*—can leave me having sleep-free nights for a week.

But you asked me The Question. You wanted to know why I don't celebrate Christmas. And this time, I'm going to tell you.

❄❄❄

Ten years ago on Christmas Eve, Vince and I had just got engaged. We'd been engaged for a week, in fact, but we were still in the process of telling our friends and families the big news.

And we were just learning one of the facts of soon-to-be-married life: we were to spend the rest of our lives in a tug-of-war between our two families. Vince's parents had been less than impressed when we said we were spending Christmas with *my* parents that year. Their consolation prizes—that we would spend New Year's at theirs, and they were the first to know about the big engagement—didn't seem to have appeased them much. On the other hand, my parents had been pleased to welcome us for the big day, but disappointed we would be gone the next morning to get back to work (and wouldn't be returning to their house for New Year). It was the classic compromise that satisfied no-one: we were spending all of our precious leave from work trying to make everyone happy and we would return, knackered and overfed, having pleased none of them. *Welcome to married life!*

Vince was a city boy. Whenever we drove out to my hometown, he would always comment on how it was "in the arse end of nowhere!", as if it was his first visit and he was shocked. But this Christmas Eve he was especially grumpy. The weather was shit and getting worse. Those country roads aren't very forgiving in the snow.

The first few flakes had us whooping like children. "It's a white Christmas!"

How many of those do we get nowadays? They seem to belong entirely in long-ago childhood memories. But as the flurries got heavier and the visibility worse, we started worrying. My hometown is, as my fiancé so delicately pointed out, in the middle of nowhere, and our little grey hatchback—we called it Bernard—was not always the most reliable car in the world.

Soon we were crawling along the ungritted country roads, Vince struggling to keep us on track.

I called my mum.

"This storm is unreal," I told her.

"What storm?" she asked. "It's clear as a bell here."

"We can barely move, Mum. I don't know if—"

"You're breaking up, love. Can you—?"

I caught the odd word after that, but soon it was just buzzing and silence. It confused me. Why would weather like this affect the signal to that extent? I hung up.

Vince was bouncing up and down in his seat as if willing the car to keep going.

"Come on, Bernard, just a little further," he was muttering. The engine spluttered, but continued on.

Soon it became impossible to go on. The snow was so heavy we couldn't see even a metre ahead of us. It was already several inches thick on what I assumed was the roadside—it was hard to tell where that was.

"Shit," breathed Vince as the car finally rolled to a stop.

We both got our phones out. No signal at all.

"Shit," I agreed.

We looked around us, hoping to see a house. We saw some lights just beyond the edge of a thick little wood close to the roadside.

"Going to have to make a break for it, sweetie," Vince said, squeezing my hand. "This is a Christmas Eve to tell the kids about, huh?"

I rolled my eyes and put on my scarf.

"Let's just hope whoever lives in that house aren't weirdos, living all the way out here. There don't seem to be any other places around."

The wind was so strong when I opened the door that it took all of my strength to climb out. Vince and I ran through the snow, heads down, nearly tripping over several times.

As we got closer, we realised it was not a house at all. It was a traditional English pub, set back a little off the road and nestled in the tall trees. Made with old-looking brickwork and faux-Tudor style black beams and white paint on its top half, it had flower baskets hanging from its eaves, though whatever was growing in them before was swamped with snow. A line of fairy lights hung above its door, still working—just—but looking rather sorry for themselves. They cast a sad, weak glow on the snow beneath them.

An old-fashioned wooden pub sign hung above its entrance. Its peeling paintwork showed a sprite-like figure glaring out from the dark trees and proclaimed the pub's name in capital letters: THE GREEN MAN.

We dashed inside and felt an instant rush of warmth. We stood on the large welcome mat, shaking the snow off our coats.

Inside, the Green Man was the quintessential pub: it had a huge, ornate wooden bar, decorated with tinsel for the season, and a few worn bar stools. There were some small wooden tables dotted around. The centrepiece was an old-fashioned fireplace, currently burning brightly. There was a snooker table in the centre of the room and a dartboard on one wall; they both looked as if they had enjoyed quite a lot of use over the years.

"Snowing outside, is it?"

The man's voice made me jump. I'd been so distracted with shaking snow off myself I hadn't noticed him standing there.

I turned to him and saw a man in his mid-30s wearing a dishevelled business suit and red tie, his sandy-coloured hair all spiky and messed up. He wasn't covered in snow, but it was clear he'd only recently made it out of the storm himself to dry off. He was grinning.

"Yeah, just a bit," I said, taking off my coat.

"Ah. Typical luck for Christmas Eve, eh? But it's OK for me—the perfect excuse to get out of visiting my in-laws!"

He winked.

"It's Luke, by the way."

Vince and I shook his hand.

"Well, guys," he said, rubbing both hands together, "who fancies a pint? A Christmas Eve lock-in seems like a plan to me."

He turned and walked towards the bar.

"Erm, not really," I said. "We're actually just waiting for the storm to die down. We're heading to my parents' house tonight and we've still got a little way to go."

Luke laughed and nodded towards the nearest window.

"You'll be waiting a while, love," he said. "That's not 'dying down' any time soon."

We couldn't argue with that. The storm was howling, making the Green Man's old windows clatter against their frames.

Vince and I exchanged looks as Luke made his way to the bar. I looked around the room. It seemed sort of cosy, sure. But spending the night here? Waking up on a boozer's sticky carpet on Christmas morning? I wasn't keen, to say the least.

Luke banged his hand on the wooden bar.

"Can we get some service out here? It's Christmas Eve night and I'm still sober!"

At first, I didn't think anyone was there. But slowly, the door behind the bar creaked open. A short man with wispy greying hair stepped out, his face gaunt and unsmiling.

"Yes?" he hissed.

Luke paused for a beat.

"Ah, merry Christmas to you as well!" he cried. "Anyway—I've broken down outside. Don't think I'll be driving tonight, and nor will these good people here. Any chance of three pints to tide us over?"

"Actually," I said, stepping forward, "I would just like to use your landline. I can't get any signal out here and my parents are expecting us—"

"You won't get through to anyone out here," the landlord interrupted. I don't think he was planning to elaborate, but when we all stared at him dumbfounded, he explained. "The phone lines are down."

"So we can't even call for help? Surely there's some way we can get through—internet access or something?" Vince pressed.

"Everything's *down*."

The landlord rested his hands on the bar and leaned towards us.

"Now. A pint each, is it?"

Vince and I walked over to the fireplace. It struck me that this was the first time in my adult life that I'd ever been properly out of reach. I remember being in town once, as a teen before the smartphone era really dawned, with my brick-like mobile phone running out of battery. I'd felt a bit like this then. But that time, I knew all I had to do was ask in a shop and I could call my parents—there might even have been some public payphones about back then. But *this*—this was proper isolation.

"I could try to get Bernard going again—make a break for the main roads," Vince offered quietly. I looked out the window. The storm was still raging, snow piling up on the windowsills.

"There's no point," I said. "I think we're stuck here for the night."

"That's the spirit!" Luke called over. He balanced three pints precariously in his hands as he made his way over to the fireside with us. "Christmas Eve lock-in! We're living the dream, guys."

We sat by the fireside and drank. The landlord skulked behind his bar, eyeing us with something like disdain. But despite this hardly being our idea of a great Christmas Eve, it did start to feel quite cosy. Maybe it was just the beer, maybe it was Luke's jolliness (which was annoying and catching in equal measure), but I was actually feeling the Christmas spirit before long. We even started singing Christmas songs—loudly and off-key.

We were halfway through 'Jingle Bells' when I saw a face pressed against the window. Something about the face's hostile expression made me jump. It was horrible, its thin lips curled into a terrible sneer. Its cold blue eyes pierced right through me as we made eye contact. The face—too small to be an adult, too full of hate to be a child—was impish and topped off by a pointed green hat.

I screamed, jumped to my feet and smashed my glass on the floor.

The hideous face moved away from the window, quick as a flash. By the time Vince had spun around to follow my gaze, it was gone.

"There was someone there!" I insisted, pointing to where I had seen him. Vince put a protective arm around my shoulders.

"Where? At the window?"

Luke ran over to the window, holding his pint protectively. He put his hand up on the glass and squinted into the snowy landscape beyond.

After a few seconds of searching, he turned back to us with a shrug.

"Nobody out there now," he said. "No footprints or anything."

I rested my head on Vince's shoulder, willing my breathing and heart rate to go back to normal.

"You sure the old demon drink isn't getting to you already?"

I wanted to snap back at Luke, but I was just so freaked out. That cold stare felt like it had burrowed into my brain.

"I know what I saw," I replied flatly.

The landlord had come out with his dustpan and brush. He was on one knee, clearing up the glass I'd smashed, muttering incoherently to himself.

"Sorry," I said meekly. He didn't reply.

We were just about to sit back down when there was a thundering banging on the door. I jumped again.

"Don't let him in!" I shouted. "It's—the thing I saw!"

"Or it could be people who need our help, eh?" Luke replied with a visible eye roll.

He sauntered over to the door—but hesitated. Clearly he wasn't dismissing what I was saying out of hand, then.

"Who is it?" he called.

"Please—our car broke down and we can't find any houses!"

We all breathed a sigh of relief.

When Luke opened the heavy pub door, he was nearly blown backwards by the force of the snowstorm. Two figures, their faces entirely covered by scarfs, ran in. They were weighed down by snow.

"Since when do we get snow like this in England?" Vince muttered.

They slammed the door shut, closing off the freezing air. Both of the newcomers took off their scarfs and started to shake themselves off. They were young looking, no older than their early 20s—one man and one woman.

"Thanks so much for letting us in," said the woman in what sounded like a Canadian accent. "We were worried we weren't going to find anywhere!"

"Do you have any rooms left?" the man asked the landlord, who was now disposing of the glass I broke. He sounded Canadian too.

"We don't have rooms. This is a pub," the landlord spat back at them.

"Oh."

"But—you can join the Christmas lock-in with the three of us!" Luke invited, gesturing grandly to the fireplace. "Beer and crap singing and absolutely no annoying relatives. Best parts of Christmas without the shit!"

The young couple exchanged glances.

"Sure," she said. "Sounds great. I'm Ella, by the way. This is Bill."

Luke treated them to their first pint of the night. I sat down on one of the seats with a view of the window, but at a safe distance. Each time I looked out there, I felt a shiver run down my spine.

II: FROSTY WINDS

The night wore on. The buzz of beer and Christmas songs started to wane. Bill and Ella were lovely enough—they told us stories of how they were over here on student visas, travelling up to spend Christmas with some friends from college on the same exchange, none of whom could afford to fly back to Canada for the festive season either.

The storm got louder and more intense. I hadn't settled after seeing that unnerving face at the window. Every logical bone in my body told me the same excuses: I'd just seen Bill peering in and my mind had played tricks; the pint had gone to my head quicker than expected; I'd let the warmth of the fire get to me and momentarily drifted off into a waking nightmare that blended with reality for a moment. After all, weren't all of these much more *logical* than the idea there was a grinning maniac in an elf's hat out there in the snow? And that was supposed to be me: level-headed, sensible Sue. Vince was the dreamer.

The landlord brought down some bedding—in various states of cleanliness, by the looks of it—and dumped it unceremoniously in the middle of the room. Something about seeing that brought it home to us. This wasn't just a temporary, weird little Christmas glitch. We really were going to wake up on Christmas morning in a boozer, lying on the sticky carpet or worn-down padded sofas, rather than surrounded by family and friends.

Vince and I chose two adjacent seats that surrounded a small booth—a snug, really, in the corner of the pub. We wrapped ourselves in blankets and put our heads down on cushions, as there were only so many pillows to go around. Bill and Ella, who happily told us such storms were ten a penny in Canada, settled down on two sofas in the bar area. Luke, who had drunk so much his words were barely coherent now, laid down by the fireplace, singing slurred versions of Christmas songs to himself.

"Where will you sleep?" I asked the landlord. "Is there a flat above the pub?"

He turned to me. Suddenly I noticed how pale he had gone.

"Merry Christmas," he rasped back. He gave a joyless smile and disappeared into the back room. I heard him lock it from the other side.

"Friendly guy," Ella said.

"At least he gave us bedding," Vince replied. "I was certain he was just going to announce 'final orders' and throw us out into the snow!"

I instinctively looked at the window where I'd seen that horrible face. Luckily, we'd agreed to pull the curtains. But despite the cosy yet budget setting, every time I thought of that window I realised how very isolated we were. None of us had signal. The landlord had put a stop to the idea of calling for help from a landline. Internet out here was non-existent. Rare nowadays to feel so genuinely alone.

Vince squeezed my hand as we settled down.

"Hopefully your parents will have called the police," he said, smiling. "They're probably looking for us. Maybe the snow has just delayed them. They might even turn up here before morning!"

"My mother will be going spare," I said. "She'll think we're dead in a ditch somewhere."

"Well then, we'll get a warm welcome when we arrive tomorrow morning."

We turned off the lights. The only light now was coming from the roaring fire. Somehow, that made me feel safer: the pub would look closed from outside, so any intruders might assume people had left and the place was locked up. Well, that sounds like a stupid line of reasoning now. But it was really all I had to comfort myself as I struggled to sleep, ignoring the blowing winds clattering the windows in their frames.

I don't know how long I slept. My dozing was fitful, full of strange dreams. By the time I jolted awake fully, everyone else was dead to the world.

I blinked a few times as my eyes adjusted to the darkness. Then I heard something that made my blood run cold: a cruel cackle.

I lay rigid-still. My heart beat so loud it nearly drowned out everything else. For a few seconds I heard nothing more, and I almost convinced myself I'd imagined it. But then it came again: a manic, horrid laugh, full of spite.

Some deep preservation instinct told me to stay still. I pulled my covers over my head like a child, leaving just a little room to peek into the pub. I battled to keep my breathing steady.

I couldn't see anyone about other than the rest of the stranded ones, asleep. But something by the door caught my eye. Water was seeping in, drenching the carpet. The wet patch was growing fast. Snow was pushing under the gap in the door as if it was being shovelled against the wood.

As I watched, the patch of water turned to ice and moved upwards. It didn't look possible at first. A block of ice was literally building itself from the ground up. Within seconds it stood four feet tall.

It began to crack. I saw it splinter apart. And there stood an elf.

This wasn't the elf of a Christmas fairytale. This wasn't some rosy-cheeked exploited worker singing as he built toys in Santa's workshop. He was dressed the part, with a very slim build, green pointed hat and green top and tiny trousers. But everything about him radiated malice. I shuddered as I recognised the same face I'd seen at the window. His expression was set in an unnaturally large grin, but it looked more like an animal showing off its aggressive fangs than a real smile. Even by the flickering light of the fire, I could make out his cold, piercing eyes. It seemed like they would turn anything they looked at to ice.

He scanned the room. When his gaze got close to me, I held my eyes tightly shut. I was too paralysed by fear to scream for help; but if I could pretend to be asleep, maybe he would move past me.

It felt like hours where I couldn't see what the monster was doing. But really, it was probably only a few seconds. Finding not knowing where he was more unbearable than watching the horror unfold, I opened my eyes again.

For a heart-stopping moment I couldn't see him. Then I found where he was: kneeling beside Luke's passed out form by the fire. He brought his face close to the sleeping man's. They would have been eyeball to eyeball if Luke had been awake.

Suddenly, the elf cackled again—a horrifying sound. Luke didn't wake up. Maybe that's what doomed him.

The elf grabbed Luke by the leg and began to lug him to the door. It must have taken supernatural strength: Luke was a big guy and had at least two feet of height on the elf. But from his jolly, bouncy movements, you wouldn't have thought the elf was carrying anything at all.

Luke moaned as he was dragged across the pub floor, head bouncing heavily on the ground. When they reached the door, the elf held up his hand. The door flew open without him even touching it. Snow flew in.

Something about the cold air hitting the pub jolted me into action.

"Luke!" I screamed, getting to my feet and rushing for the door. "Don't take him! No!"

But it was too late: with one final, horrible cackle, the elf and his victim had disappeared into the snow. By the time I reached the door, it had slammed shut again.

I tried to pull it open, but it was frozen shut. Screaming, I started to bang on the wood.

The commotion woke up Vince and the students. Within seconds, all three were around me. Vince put a protective hand on my shoulder.

"What the fuck—?"

"It's Luke!" I shouted. "That—*thing* took him! Dragged him out into the snow as if it was nothing."

I had one more go at opening the door. No luck. The ice had it stuck like glue. The only sign that anything had opened it recently was the soggy patch of wet carpet by the door.

"What thing?"

"That thing I saw at the window! That elf thing!"

Ella and Bill exchanged a meaningful look. Vince tried to look concerned, but I could see the relief flooding him: *ah*, he was thinking, *she's just had another nightmare. Luke's probably just out having a cigarette somewhere.* It infuriated me.

"I'm not fucking crazy! Or dreaming, or making it up, or—"

I didn't finish my sentence. There was a huge crash just outside the door that made us all jump backwards.

Ella scanned the room. Her eyes settled on an old-fashioned poker by the fire—a heavy bronze-coloured object. She grabbed it and held it in front of her with both hands, like a heavy sword.

"Let's stick close together and go and see what that was," she said.

We let her lead the way. Behind her, the three of us held up our phones—useless for calling for help without signal but useful in torch mode. Bill moved past her, put his shoulder against the door, and pushed. It took a few thrusts, but eventually it blew open. The storm was violent as ever; the snow just would not stop.

Our phone lights all converged on the horrible sight on the Green Man's doorstep. Luke was lying there on his back, stripped down to his underwear apart from the Santa hat on his head, arms and legs tied together in front of him with flashing Christmas lights. I screamed and stumbled backwards.

Vince ran forwards and put his fingers to Luke's neck. He jolted his hand away almost instantly.

"He's frozen solid!"

I took a few faltering steps forward. I focused on Luke's face: his dead eyes were frozen wide open, as if he had seen something beyond words before he passed.

The lights that bound Luke were still flashing and buzzing, despite not being plugged in to any power. He had an oversized red bauble saying "Happy Holidays" shoved in his mouth. It was stuffed so deep into him that only the message and the tip of the bauble showed.

But his hands caught my eye. The fingernails were all cracked and bloodied, as if he had been dragged somewhere and tried to claw his way out frantically. One set of fingers was clasped on to a folded piece of paper.

As soon as I noticed it, I heard that bone-chilling cackle once again. It seemed to come from everywhere at once, echoing across the clearing and through the trees.

Ella and Bill stepped past Luke's body, Ella holding the brass poker aloft.

"Come out here you fucking coward!" Bill shouted. "Bet you won't take us all on at once!"

His threat seemed to make the elf hysterical. His cackling got even louder and more deranged.

I couldn't take my eyes off the paper in Luke's dead hand.

"Go ahead, go ahead! *Take it,*" the voice hissed, menacing and mocking in equal measure. All eyes were suddenly on me.

"Darling—don't," Vince advised softly.

But I couldn't resist. I reached down and prized the paper away. One of his fingers made a sickening crack, like a whipping sound, and snapped off. I let it fall away and retched. This sent the elf into spasms of laughter. Bill and Ella scanned the clearing, trying to work out where the noises were coming from.

With shaking hands, I unfolded the paper. Vince put his phone light over my shoulder so I could see.

The note was scrawled in jagged handwriting I could barely read. But when I puzzled it out, I felt sick.

It said: *"GUESS WHAT, SUE? I KNEW YOU WERE AWAKE AND WATCHING ME WHEN I TOOK HIM."*

I let the note drop to the floor and dashed back into the Green Man, the elf's cackles ringing in my ears.

III: SNOW ON SNOW

Vince followed me in. Ella and Bill came in after us. I wiped the tears from my eyes.

"We need to lock ourselves in the cellar," I insisted. "If we can survive until morning, live through this storm, we might have a chance against him."

The fire was starting to die down, leaving the pub almost dark except for the gentle twinkling of the fairy lights at the windows.

I pulled myself over the bar and started to hammer on the door the landlord had disappeared into some time ago.

"Hey! Someone's dead! Get out here right now!"

No sound. Nothing stirred on the other side.

Vince asked me to move back and kicked the door in. It took three attempts—it was an old-fashioned, heavy wooden one—but it eventually gave out. As the door slammed off its hinges, we heard that disgusting cackle again. It seemed to be coming from everywhere at once, all around us, from the pub and from outside together.

Then came the footsteps. It sounded like the elf had somehow landed on the roof. He scuttled from one end of the Green Man's roof to the other. Though his spider-like movements were light, each step landed absurdly heavily, sending a cloud of dust and plaster to the floor.

"The cellar!" I repeated.

We packed into the small dark corridor behind the bar. No sign of the landlord—but that didn't particularly worry me. I saw the entrance to the cellar not far from the first door. Anything to get us further away from the elf seemed like a good idea, even if we were cornering ourselves underground.

I flicked the light switch. Thank goodness the light still worked. It lit up the steep stairs leading into the cave-like cellar beneath the Green Man.

It was surprisingly large for a relatively small, rural pub. There were several wooden cases of wine covering two whole whitewashed walls of the room. They were grouped by country of origin: Italy, France, Australia. Beyond that, there were kegs of all different types of beers. They had stickers on them saying the name of the ale: some were recognisable, some seemed to be home brewed. The one nearest the front was labelled "Green Man's Glory". For a guy who had been kind of hostile about selling us anything at all, the landlord sure owned a lot of alcohol.

"At least we'll die drunk down here," said Ella. "Happy Christmas indeed!"

"Don't talk like that," snapped Bill. "We can't start thinking like that. And I'm damned if I'm gonna let some murderous fucking Christmas elf push us around."

He took the poker out of Ella's hands.

"When that little shit comes down here after us, I'm ready for him."

No sooner were the words out of his mouth than we heard the elf's hysterical laughter. It was so close it made us jump; it seemed to be coming from just beyond the cellar door. Bill swallowed hard and held the poker above his head, as if ready to strike it down on the elf's head the second he appeared.

"So scared, Billy boy, so scared!" the elf exclaimed, then fell back into fits of sinister giggles.

"Yeah? Well come and face me then, you fucking coward!"

The laughter stopped abruptly. The lights flickered, making us all huddle together like frightened children in the centre of the room. The silence... it seemed to drag on for hours. Nothing but the sound of our frantic breathing.

We all had our eyes fixed on the top of the stairs, expecting the elf to rush in and attack us at any moment.

When he popped up behind us, appearing suddenly from behind one of the wine racks, it was too late for us to react.

"Surprise!" he cried, picking up a huge metal keg of beer as if it was light as a feather.

Bill just had time to spin on his heel and lunge towards the creature, poker drawn like a sword. But the elf heaved the keg through the air with superhuman strength. It smashed into the centre of Bill's face with a sickening crunch. As he stumbled backwards, he stepped through the light. It looked like his nose had been flattened against the rest of his face. His features were a sick mess of gore and bone, except for his eyes, which were widened in agony and dazed from the blow.

He fell backwards heavily. The back of his head cracked on the bottom step and he slumped, motionless.

The only sounds in that cellar were the triumphant cackling of the elf and an inhuman roar of despair from Ella. She rushed to his side, kneeling down and cradling the bloodied mess that had once been Bill's head in her hands. She threw back her head and screamed.

Seeming to teleport across the room, the elf appeared at his other side. With lightning quick reactions, he grabbed the fire poker and held it over his head, like Bill had held it minutes before.

"Merry Christmas!" he laughed.

He brought the pointed end of the poker down on Ella's neck. It sliced through her throat and spine like a knife through butter. He pushed it down with such force that the end of it, once through her flesh, burrowed several inches into the stone floor. It left her propped up that way by her pierced neck, her body convulsing, disgusting gurgling noises coming from her mouth as bubbles of blood burst out on to her chin and top.

Vince tugged my arm urgently, jolting me away from the horrifying spectacle. He dragged me along with him for the first few steps until my legs dutifully started to accept the frenzied instructions to *run like hell* that my brain was sending them.

We darted up the stairs. Halfway up, I couldn't resist one final glance back at the elf.

He was standing between the two bodies, watching us with his tiny hands on his hips as if amused by our escape. Once again, my eyes met his cold, evil stare. He raised one hand and gave a slow, sarcastic wave. I turned away and continued to run.

We slammed the cellar door shut and ran back towards the bar. I started shouting for the landlord to get out of the pub.

"Fuck him," Vince said. "He knew that *thing* was in the woods. He let it come for us."

We reached the bar area. I ran for the door and was shocked when Vince didn't follow. Instead, he broke a leg off a pub chair by smashing it into a table. He took the jagged leg and shoved it into the slowly dying fire. It caught light instantly.

He ran it across the curtains first. They were set ablaze right away. Then he set fire to the rest of the furniture. In no time at all, the bar area was a blazing inferno.

He threw the burning chair leg through the door behind the bar in the direction of the cellar that still, presumably, held the elf.

We smashed our way through the door. Surprisingly, it was sunrise; I'd lost track of time in the horror. The snowstorm was easing off, replaced by an almost mockingly calm and beautiful morning sunshine.

Vince and I held each other as we ran away. When we were at a safe distance, we both collapsed on the ground and lay in the snow, hoping to watch the Green Man and the evil it harboured go up in flames, never to hurt another person.

But the pub was intact. No sign of the blazing fire we'd started just moments before.

The landlord appeared at our side, making us both scream and struggle to our feet.

"Congratulations," he said. "He doesn't always leave survivors. You must have caught him at a time of real Christmas spirit."

"I'll give you fucking Christmas spirit—"

Vince started towards him, but I held him back. The landlord cracked a smile, the first I'd seen from him. I didn't want to see what happened if you tried to hit this prick. Who knows, maybe he could teleport too? He'd certainly appeared beside us suddenly.

"What *was* that thing?"

The landlord sighed.

"I don't know where he came from. I know that elf thing is only his preferred form. He must be—what? A demon? I don't think there's a word for it. He turned up one Christmas and massacred my entire pub. My whole family. He only let me live on one condition."

We waited for him to say something. He didn't. But I realised I already knew what he meant.

"You keep running the pub and you give him victims," I muttered.

He nodded, avoiding my eyes.

"That was twenty years ago. If I do my bit at Christmas, he lets me live a normal life the rest of the year. Come tomorrow, the pub will appear in a different town. Everyone will act as if it's a beloved local they've visited for decades. They'll greet me like an old friend and ask what night the pub quiz is, and if we serve scampi. It's bliss."

He sighed again and lowered his eyes.

"But I really fucking hate Christmas."

"You selfish fuck," Vince spat at him.

"Hmm. Probably fair. But you don't know what he's capable of. Killing people is the most merciful thing he does."

He started to walk back towards the Green Man.

"Have a good Christmas, both of you, won't you?" he called over his shoulder.

As he closed the door to his pub, another sudden flurry of snow picked up, momentarily covering our eyes. When we blinked it away, it calmed down as quickly as it had arrived. Neither of us were surprised to see an empty clearing between the trees where the Green Man had stood when our eyesight returned to normal.

We didn't speak as we walked back to Bernard the car. I got into the driver's seat. It started on the first attempt.

I did a three point turn in the road, heading back to our home in the city. Later, I'd ring my parents; I'd explain we'd broken down and had to cancel the trip. I'd suggest New Year's instead, and we'd visit Vince's parents the weekend after. We'd break the news of our engagement. Just a small family wedding, I'd explain; no big celebrations, no decorations, no theme. Next Christmas, I'd say we were going abroad instead. There would always, always be an excuse not to "do Christmas" from now on.

The snow was melting into a slush remarkably quickly. The sun was unseasonably warm and bright.

As we drove back towards our home, I reached across and clasped Vince's hand in mine. We would never have to explain to one another why our house would be free of Santa, decorations, trees, and elves every December of our married life.

Until now, I've told no-one. Even Vince and I don't speak of it often together. Strange, isn't it? You'd think we would be questioning it together forever, driven mad by the mystery of it. Sometimes repressing these things is actually healthy, I think. It's still there, of course. It's there in how we quickly switch off the TV and radio whenever a Christmas ad comes on (earlier and earlier each year, I swear). It's there when we're in the garden centre and we both catch each other's eyes as we walk, head down, through the Christmas decorations section. It's always there at the edges of our minds, cackling away.

A few months ago, we discovered we were expecting our first child. We're delighted. But I wonder if the kid will even make it to pre-school before asking The Question: "Mummy, Daddy—why don't we celebrate Christmas?"

Flashing Plastic Lights

William always wanted what I had, only better. He'd been like it since we were kids.

Growing up in the same small town, our different circumstances were only too clear. William's family was rich compared to mine, and he wanted to prove that fact constantly. If I got a bike, he'd turn up the next week with a bigger one that cost twice as much. He'd arrive at school in designer clothes and ask me where I got mine, smirking as I tried to avoid telling him they were from a secondhand shop.

I thought this trait of his would get better as he got older, but he only got more competitive. I tried to distance myself from him but that was hard in such a small, isolated place. He moved to the city after a few years and frankly, I was glad to be rid of him. Nothing about this supposed friendship was fulfilling to me, and he was never there to celebrate my achievements or commiserate when times were hard.

I married Mary, my school years sweetheart. I qualified as a phlebotomist and settled into a stable, mostly happy life. We lived in a quiet cul-de-sac in a modest two-bedroom house. We tried for kids, but it didn't happen for us.

Years slipped by like someone sliding downwards in a hot, steamy bath. Once a year, we'd decorate the outside of the house for Christmas. We went all out—we just liked it that way—and our little display started to get attention. We added a waving, light-up Santa to the roof one year. The next we doubled the number of fairy lights and gave Santa a light-up sleigh and set of reindeer. Our garden became an overwhelming feast for the eyes, full of flashing lights and primary colours. The electricity bills were eye-watering, but it made people happy.

Mary and I started to look forward to it. As more people came to see our light show, we started taking charity collections for the local hospice. Kids began calling our house "the Christmas house", all year round, which made me oddly proud. We took out sweets and hot drinks for the assembled crowds. Those dark December nights in a scarf and heavy-duty coat were among the happiest of my life.

Our neighbours across the cul-de-sac never complained, but when I saw the "For Sale" sign outside their house I'll admit I got a bit nervous. What if their replacements complained about the lights, the noise, the people?

The neighbours moved out in early November. As soon as I saw the flashy new car parked behind the van outside on moving in day, I got a sick feeling in my stomach. The house was significantly larger than ours, and only a select few people could afford a property like that.

William grinned like a child on Christmas morning when he leaped out of his car and saw me.

"Ted!" he shouted, swaggering towards me with his arms outstretched as if we were long-lost old friends. Self-awareness was never William's strong point, so maybe he actually thought we were.

I tried not to look devastated and dutifully answered his probing questions, masquerading as small talk.

"Of course I'll still be commuting to the city on the regular," he said airily. "They gave me a huge pay-rise when I said I was thinking of leaving. They were so desperate to keep me, they agreed to let me do most of my work from home! They said they couldn't replace talent like mine. Anyway Ted—what do you do nowadays?"

"I'm a phlebotomist," I replied, my voice sounding hoarse. I mimed drawing blood out of an arm. "I work at the hospital."

"Ah! Pay well, does it?"

All the old resentment, long buried, came swirling back like a tornado. Luckily I was saved by the sound of the delivery man knocking on my own house's door, balancing a huge box between his arms and on his knee.

"Got to go, William," I said, already walking across to my side of the street. "Latest Christmas decoration delivery's here!"

A strange look passed across William's face when I said this, but he soon recovered and forced his usual film star, plastered-on smile.

"We'll catch up later then! Got lots of expensive furniture to move in and I don't trust the removal team to do it without me watching."

I succeeded in avoiding William for the next few days. If we ever bumped into each other, I would quickly make an excuse—work, family obligation—and hurry away. But there was only so long I could keep it up. I spent my evenings gloomily looking at property websites, fantasising about packing it all in and moving to New Zealand instead. For all I knew, William would probably follow us there.

Mary tried to distract me by focusing on the Christmas decorations. Every time I got back from work, she'd tell me excitedly about the latest deliveries, the new baubles and tinsel.

As mid-November approached, we put up the beginnings of the display. Slowly, the whole thing began to take shape. It was magnificent, by far the most ambitious one we'd done so far. The fun of spending quality time with Mary took my mind off our irritating new neighbour. I found myself laughing again, enjoying all our little in-jokes as we put the finishing touches to our annual masterpiece.

Santa and his bigger-than-man size sleigh were the last to go up. I stood on the roof, fiddling with the wiring—until movement over at William's house caught my eye.

He was standing in the road, hands on hips, loudly directing a group of three workers as they assembled a basic scaffolding across the front of his house.

That same familiar feeling of rage started to bubble in my guts.

"William!" I shouted from the roof. He turned to me, shit-eating grin there already, pretending he hadn't seen me. "What's going on?"

"Oh, this stuff? I know a guy from the city whose company does outdoor Christmas displays. They do all the best hotels. Trust me—they're the greatest! Anyway, he owed me a favour so I thought I might bring a bit of festive cheer to this old town."

I felt my nails digging into my palm, hand clasped around the wires. My legs felt unstable.

William gestured to my house.

"I see you like Christmas yourself! Well, nothing like a bit of friendly competition, is there?"

He laughed and went back to ordering the workers around.

Somehow, I managed to make it down from the roof and back into my house before vomiting. Mary tried to console me but there was nothing she could do.

I didn't work on the display for a week. I took time off work and spent each day by the window, watching the construction of William's Christmas display. Its magnificence was unquestionable. No way I could ever compete with that. He'd won—again.

By the third day of my absence from work, I knew what I had to do. And it had nothing to do with any petty fantasies about sabotaging his lights, so he looked stupid on launch night. No—he'd declared war, and that was what he was going to get.

The crowds in the cul-de-sac were the biggest ever that year. They were swelled slightly by the large amounts of emergency service personnel and both local and national TV crews but hey, they all count!

It wasn't William's gaudy, paint-by-numbers corporate display they were all looking at. It was ours. They were pointing at Santa's sleigh, hands over their mouths. Some were recording on their phones as the police tried in vain to keep them back from the scene.

I went quietly, of course. Let them slap the handcuffs on me and read me my rights without complaint. I hummed some of my favourite Christmas carols as they ran through it all. The hardest part was Mary, sobbing furiously next to me. She kept repeating "what have you done?!" and dissolving into a howling mess. It was irritating. I'd finally managed to get our display next-level attention and this was how she thanked me.

As they led me away from the house, there was so much shouting. Press screaming questions, popping their camera flash at me. One or two angry people telling me that I was scum. None of it worried me. I carried on humming festive tunes as they hurried me to the car. I was pleased to see every eye on me at that moment. William was there, on full display as it were, but for once everyone turned to me rather than him.

I got one final glance at my masterpiece as they bundled me into the back of the police car. William's dead body was dressed in a Santa hat, squashed into the sleigh, kept upright by the Christmas tree I'd forced up his anus until the tip poked out of his mouth—that took some doing, let me tell you. I'd wrapped an entire line of fairy lights around his neck tightly, and amazingly, they still seemed to be flashing.

I looked at my former friend's dead face, for once not in control, for once shocked and helpless. Merry Christmas, dickhead.

Midnight Mass

Religion's not really my thing.

In fact, I can think of a million and one things I'd rather be doing at 11pm on Christmas Eve night than heading to a religious service with my grandma. She brought me up after my folks died when I was a baby, and it's mostly been fine. But she's forced me to every faith event going my whole life. I'm not even sure I believe anymore. Not that I'd ever dare tell her that, obviously.

I'm slouched in the back of the car, scowling as I watch us get further from the centre of town.

"Take that face off you, young man," Grandma scolds me. Even at 80, she can sound fierce when she wants to.

"Grandma, can you just drop me off in town? I'll get a drink and wait for you."

"No! You'll come and show respect to our Lord. While you live under my roof, you obey my rules."

I do a quick calculation in my head. In two years' time I'll be 18 and out of here. Drinking my Christmas Eves away like normal people.

Despite Grandma's exceptionally slow driving, we eventually get to that old, familiar place of worship I've come to know so well over the years. People are already filing in. One or two wave to Grandma as they pass our car. Some are already wearing their robes.

I decide to appeal to her one last time.

"Grandma," I say, "it's Christmas Eve! Can't you just—"

She spins around in her chair as if she's suffered an electric shock. Her eyes are wild and furious.

"Shut up! Don't you *dare* use that blasphemous word!"

I'm shocked by the venom in her voice.

"Gr—Grandma—" I start, but she doesn't want to hear it.

"Not a word more! Do you know how much this family has sacrificed for this faith? You'll get inside and worship our Lord! There are so many blasphemers out tonight, celebrating their disgusting services. We need to let our Lord know he is very much in *our* hearts, tonight more than ever!"

What choice do I have? I get out of the car and walk in with her.

The pentagram is already set up. Most of our family friends are there, kneeling, praying their Hail Satans. A girl I used to go to religion classes with throws up a friendly devil horns sign with her hand as I pass her. I half-heartedly return it, wishing I could be in town with my school friends instead.

This year's sacrifices are already tied up and gagged. The man is struggling, but the woman has her eyes closed in ecstasy. It is, according to our faith—Grandma's faith—the highest honour to die this way. Their newborn squeals in the cot next to them. Every year, at what "the blasphemers" call Christmas, one family is chosen by the community to be sacrificed, their baby baptised to the Lord of Death in their lifeblood. 16 years ago it was my parents. It bestows high honour upon the infant, being orphaned during Midnight Black Mass, ensuring their faith in Satan never be tested. I wonder why it didn't work on me?

The priest raises the holy machete, speaking in tongues, honouring Satan. Just before it comes down on the man's throat, our eyes meet for a split second. I think I see fear there. Doubt. Maybe he sees the same in me. Our little, final, futile secret: all of this is nonsense.

Mistletoe-ho-ho

Did you know mistletoe's a parasite? Well, technically only a half-parasite; it can photosynthesise too. But it gets most of its resources from the trees it latches on to. It steals their nutrients so it can grow.

It isn't really the jolly, innocent Christmas plant we make it out to be, despite the pretty berries. Birds carry it around and it lands on trees through their droppings. Then it sort of burrows into the tree branches and feeds off them. It's evergreen, so even when the tree is barren in winter, the mistletoe just keeps spreading and thriving, greener than ever.

I learnt this on my first day as Assistant Gardener at the city park. In fact, it was the first thing my boss, Margaret, taught me.

"Mistletoe. Gotta watch out for mistletoe, Sasha," she told me, tapping her fingers on the table for emphasis. "Mistletoe's a *cancer*."

Margaret was a kindly middle-aged woman, and what my parents would have called "a character". She had an odd turn of phrase and though she *really* knew her stuff about the park and plants, it was hard to hold a conversation with her about anything else. I liked her, sure, but as an eighteen-year-old in my first job out of school, she wasn't really my first choice of colleague. Not that I would have told her that.

One thing we did have in common was our love of the outdoors. And the city park was *beautiful*. I couldn't have asked for a better place to work. Acres of parkland, a range of perfectly looked-after trees, and plenty of money to experiment with floral displays in the spring and summer.

As I settled in, I felt more at ease speaking to Margaret about my life outside of work. We'd be pruning hedges or repotting plants, and I would be twittering away about my boyfriend, my next planned family holiday or whatever else was on my mind that day. She never said anything about her own life. And when I spoke, she usually responded with "uh-huh" or some other slightly bored noise. But I kept confiding. It didn't seem right to me that we'd been working together for months and just didn't know anything about each other.

"I'm introducing Tom to my family this Christmas," I told her once as we were weeding a flower bed.

"Oh, right," she said, not looking up from her weeding.

"I'm a bit nervous. Hope they like each other!"

"Hmm."

"Erm—do *you* have any plans this Christmas, Margaret?"

Silence. For a moment, I thought she was going to ignore me. I'd broken the unwritten rule.

"No," she muttered finally.

We pulled weeds quietly beside each other for a few moments. I tugged up a huge one.

"Look at the roots on that!" I exclaimed.

She laughed.

"Wow! Nice one, Sasha. It's really important to get those deep-rooted ones."

And the equilibrium, at least for that day, was restored. It was a couple of days later when she first mentioned the mistletoe infestation.

The bus was late, so I reached the park a bit later than usual. Margaret greeted me at the entrance, looking concerned.

"Mistletoe! We've got mistletoe," she told me. "Bloody monstrous, cuckoo-like plant it is. Sucks all the life out of perfectly good trees."

"Oh no," I said. "Where is it?"

"I've got it down. Got rid of it. But it'll be back. We need to watch these trees like hawks, Sasha. Hawks!"

We had three more outbreaks of "the demon parasite", as Margaret colourfully christened it, within a week. Margaret's demeanour started to get noticeably less friendly. I'd hear her mumbling to herself as she worked. She started making more mistakes—nothing huge, but stuff she shouldn't have been missing as an experienced gardener.

But what started to strike me as odd was that I was never there when she caught it. She always moaned about finding it just after I'd returned from my lunch break, or when she was working extra hours either in the morning or at night (which wasn't a rare occurrence). Maybe I just should have left it well alone. But the more it happened, the weirder it seemed, and the more my curiosity grew.

"I've just ripped down another clump of mistletoe!" she exclaimed once when I walked into the park at 7am one frosty December morning. "Horrible stuff, pointless stuff—"

"Did you throw it away?" I asked, trying to keep my voice light.

"Yes..."

"Which bin did you put it in? It's just that I'd like to keep some—you know, for Christmas decorations. It may as well be some use, right? And since Tom's coming round for Christmas this year, it would have its own uses hanging above the door."

Margaret instantly retreated into her shell. She shook her head.

"You don't want to be going through bins for mistletoe. They sell it at the market for a few pennies, if that's your sort of thing."

She didn't mention mistletoe again that day. But she didn't speak much at all. I worried I'd upset or embarrassed her. Maybe she was making up the mistletoe—but perhaps she just wanted to teach me how dangerous it was? Or to make it sound like there was more going on in the park when I wasn't there than there really was? Or—or—or... none of it made sense. I felt pretty guilty all day, working with her side-by-side silently, wishing I hadn't said anything.

The next morning, Margaret didn't appear at work. It was the first day off sick she'd taken all year (against my nine sick days, some of which may well have been due to hangovers. But hey, I was eighteen). She didn't ring me on my mobile but left an answerphone message on the landline in our small shed-like office. I checked the time: she'd called in before I was due at work anyway. Her voice sounded distant, certainly ill, though she didn't give any indication what was wrong with her. I hoped it was nothing serious.

She turned up the next morning. I was shocked to see the state of her. She was never the most glamour-conscious person—being an outdoorsy sort like myself, it wasn't really top of the agenda—but this was something else entirely. Her eyes were framed by thick black bags. She didn't look like she'd slept at all. Her hair hadn't been washed or brushed and her face was flushed.

"Hey, Margaret—are you sure you're OK to work?"

"Yes, yes," she said, flapping her hand as if to dismiss my concerns. "I think it's safe to leave the house now. But just to warn you—it's *spreading*."

I looked back at her, bewildered.

"You mean your illness is catching? I'll stay well back—"

"No! It's the mistletoe," she leaned in close to me and whispered the rest conspiratorially, "it spread to my house."

I checked her face for signs she was winding me up. Nothing. Margaret wasn't really the joking kind.

"Well... that sounds... bad," I replied, struggling over each word. "But Margaret... usually mistletoe only grows on trees?"

"No, no, it's spreading everywhere! I found some in my shower. Then hanging over my bed. I think it was trying to grow over me while I was asleep, trying to smother me."

OK. Now I was really worried.

"Are you *sure* you're OK, Margaret? I think you might have a bit of a fever or something. Maybe a doctor could help?"

"Doctors know nothing about gardening! Not until they retire, anyway. But I've hacked it all back at home with a big knife. It's gone—for now. But that bastard weed always grows back. Nasty little parasite."

She turned on her heel and walked to the equipment shed, ready to start the day. I was left staring after her in disbelief.

Maybe I should have done more. Maybe I should have broached the subject again. But I was quite relieved when she turned her attention back to her comfort zone, the gardening, and she seemed normal and cheerful enough as she worked. By lunch time, I had rationalised it to myself that maybe her sickness had given her weird nightmares or minor hallucinations and she hadn't sufficiently recovered yet to see them for what they were. We'd probably laugh about her delusions of magical killer mistletoe when she was better!

Besides, the park was closing to the public for a few days that afternoon to give us staff members a Christmas break. So it's safe to say my mind was a little bit "elsewhere" as we completed the last few wintery tasks our roles demanded.

At the end of the day, she thanked me for all my hard work over the past few months and we wished each other a Merry Christmas. She seemed better, or at least I told myself she did—there had been no mention of the dreaded M-word since that strange encounter in the morning.

The next time I heard from Margaret, it was on the special day itself. I was just settling down to Christmas dinner with my family. Tom had settled in well and I was feeling content and full of the joys of the season. Until I read her text: *"Sasha. The mistletoe's back. Worse than ever."*

I read the words over and over. Finally, feeling completely unsure of how to handle this, I sent her back: *"Merry Christmas, Margaret. Hope you're enjoying the day! X"* Maybe playing along with her delusions would just encourage them?

A couple of hours passed. We were playing charades and getting increasingly sloshed. I'm surprised I heard my phone vibrate over the noise. My heart sank when I saw it was from Margaret.

"*It's going to get me. I can't fight it. Thank you for being a friend this past year, Sasha. X*"

Even in my inebriated state, I knew that wasn't a good sign.

I filled in my family and Tom. Told them I was calling the police and would go round to Margaret's place. They wanted to come with me, but I hoped this would just be a quick visit to check she was OK—maybe to get her to the hospital if that's what she needed.

She only lived a few blocks away, and I jogged there. I waited outside in the cold for the officers to arrive. Margaret's house was cosy, almost cottage-like, just outside the centre of the city.

The police officers came before long—two ladies who looked like they'd had a long night dealing with drunks. Perhaps a simple welfare check made a nice change!

I hung back a bit as they inspected the house. They looked into the windows and tried to peer through the letterbox.

"Can you hear that groaning?" one said to the other. The second officer nodded. That was all they needed: there was now enough confirmed concern to break in.

They kicked the door down and ran in, shouting Margaret's name. I followed along behind.

The first thing I noticed were the beige walls. There had been, at some point, some attempt to decorate them for Christmas. But they had all been slashed to ribbons. There were long, deep gouge marks in the plaster. Somebody had been hacking at them. The floor was covered in cut up snippets of tinsel. As we moved further in, I saw the staircase: the bannister had been slashed repeatedly.

I heard the moaning then. A low, pained sound.

"Margaret! We hear you! Where are you?!"

But as soon as I shouted it, I saw her. The three of us crowded around Margaret. She was slumped on the ground in the doorway of her lounge. Her face was covered in blood. In her hand, she held something hairy and pulpy, also caked in blood.

Her eyes were struggling to focus. When they saw me, they fixed on my face and she smiled.

"I got it, Sasha!" she said, between bloody coughs. "I got the damned mistletoe. It was going to kill me, but I stopped it spreading!"

She held the crimson, dripping mess in her hand up towards me. And that's when my brain put the puzzle of the whole horrific scene together. The reason her head was covered in blood was because she'd hacked off her own scalp. From the looks of the jagged cuts on her forehead, it seemed to have taken several excruciating attempts. The knife was discarded by her side, clumps of skin and hair still stuck to its blade.

"I got, Sasha! *I got it!*" she shouted, and fell down on her back, her body shaking from delirious giggles.

SNOW ON SNOW

I trudge along the icy road, shivering. I don't remember what warmth feels like.

Snow on snow on snow. It just keeps falling. Usually that would be a wonderful happening late on Christmas Eve night. But now it seems to be smothering me. Have I seen a white Christmas before tonight? I don't recall. But then I'm so cold, I'm having trouble remembering my own name.

I'm on a dirt road between two endless fields. I can't tell what's growing in the fields; they're blanketed in white. I can see some farm buildings in the distance but they're empty. No other signs of life.

I'm staggering from one side of the road to the other. Everything's blurry. I taste blood in my mouth. The merciless chill in the air pervades so deep within me, it has a freezing grip on my soul.

Something keeps me walking on through this cold hellscape, even though my legs want to collapse. Call it the will to live, maybe.

How did I even get here?

I close my eyes against the wind, momentarily frightened they might freeze shut. The truth falls on me piece by piece, like snowflakes. I remember the office Christmas party. That warm pub, decked out with all the jovial signs of the season. The usual suspects: those who kept checking their watches, who left after the meal was done (sensible choice). The ones who ended up ruining the atmosphere by arguing; Terry from marketing and Lisa from quality assurance, I'm looking at you. The people who kept bringing up work topics when it was Christmas fucking Eve and we all wanted to get through this as painlessly as possible and get back to our families. And, of course, the people who drank too much. Like me. I'm always in that group.

I slip on a patch of black ice and land badly on my knee. Pain shoots through the left side of my body. I'm glad of it. It takes my mind off the cold.

I feel like a fragile skeleton made of ice, ready to shatter at any moment. The sheer cold has penetrated my entire being. I lie on the ground and momentarily consider staying there. But I know I can't. Something is driving me on.

I pull myself shakily to my feet.

All of a sudden, images are shooting through my head at top speed. *Leaving the Christmas party. Staggering to my car. Kelly from accounts asking if I was sure I could drive. Me laughing at the question, insisting I hadn't had much to drink at all. Her hesitating, looking back at the restaurant, and eventually relenting and getting in the passenger seat.*

I'm crying. *Why why why why why.* I want to go back to that moment, scream at myself to call a taxi instead. I'm surprised the tears don't freeze on my cheeks.

I'm not sure how long I stand there, regret filling me up as much as the cold. But when I see car headlights approaching, it snaps me out of my reverie.

I hobble into the centre of the road. The snow is nearly knee-deep now.

"Stop!" I shout, even though the car is still far away. It's going slowly, taking the road at a sensible pace for the conditions.

Flashes of my own crashed car go past my eyes. I just can't stop these intrusive memories.

The car was damaged but not horrifically so. But Kelly... Kelly wasn't wearing a seatbelt. Kelly's eyes were glazed. There was no life behind them. The injury on her head didn't look bad enough to kill her. But there we were.

Swallowing back more tears, I hold up my shaking hand and hold it out like a hitchhiker. The headlights get brighter. I hear the engine struggling to keep going.

"Help! I crashed my car and—and my friend is really hurt!"

Getting some energy from somewhere, I start to raise my hands above my head and wave them manically. I try to fight back more flashbacks to the crash.

Kelly was dead and there was no denying it. No taking it back now. I hesitated for only a few moments. If I call for help, I'll go to prison for drunk driving. No sense in ruining two lives just for a simple mistake, right? Would Kelly even want that? Before I knew what I was really doing, I opened her car door. Pulled out her corpse. Dragged it to the woods nearby. By the time the snow melted and people found her, there would be nothing left to link to my car. No one saw me offer her a lift from the office party, or so I hope. Christmas can still be OK. I'll go back to my family and act like nothing happened.

I wail with pain. The memories, the cold. The headlights are very close now.

"Please save me!" I scream. "I've killed someone! I've killed my friend!"

The car is upon me now. And in the blink of an eye, it's passed right through me. I feel nothing but a weird empty sensation.

I can see the back end of the car now, its rear lights disappearing slowly but surely towards the relative safety of town. And suddenly I remember it all.

After dumping Kelly's body, I got back in the driving seat. The car, to my surprise, still started fine. A nagging voice in the back of my head told me I could still turn back, still make this OK, admit it all to the police. But I drove away.

I was still drunk, though. Drunk and high on horrified adrenaline. Swearing and driving too fast for the conditions, I slid on a patch of ice and wrapped my already damaged car around a tree.

I stand still in the middle of the road, watching the snow fall. It seems a little lighter now. By morning, it might have eased off. Kids will wake up to a white Christmas, open their presents and set out for a magical afternoon building snowmen. Families will gather to enjoy the best day of the year. But not mine and not Kelly's.

I'll never see morning. I know that now. Twenty-five years since the crash on that fateful Christmas Eve and I relive it, over and over again. Christmas Day is still waiting, just out of reach forever.

This is my punishment. I had the chance to do the right thing but instead I threw my friend's body into the woods for the animals to eat and sped away. And because of that I'll spend eternity in the cold, trying in vain to make amends for my actions. Redemption, like Christmas morning, will be longed for but never arrive.

I sit in the snow. I'm shaking and making a hoarse sound but I'm not sure if I'm crying, laughing, or dying once again. Maybe all three. I can feel this half-life slipping out of me, but the realisation brings no relief. Death holds no peace for the likes of me.

I'll just find myself on this frigid path again, stumbling around in the snow.

The Tinsel Murders

People think true crime writing is a glamorous job. And it is, when it isn't swallowing you whole into its dark heart.

There's an old true crime cliché: "the husband did it!" You know, ninety-nine times out of a hundred, the husband *did* do it. Or the boyfriend. Or the wife, girlfriend, lover. We're addicted to the stories where the fantastical happened—the never-caught serial killers or the unlikely victims dying ten stories up in an abandoned building where the security cameras didn't pick up anything else. We like drama and intrigue. But most of the time? You have a body and the person closest to their heart stopped that heart. Usually for some dumb reason like sex, jealousy or greed. Most murders are not only a shocking waste of life, they're boring as fuck.

The rare exceptions attract the human mind like flies around, umm, sugar. But hey, I'm not judging. I tried to make a living as a literary writer before I turned to true crime and guess which one pays better? I profit off it, I mean, so I have no room to sneer at it.

Truth be known, I very rarely make an emotional connection with the cases I write about. I like it better that way. I can write about the blood and gore, the sick details we all crave, then move on to the next without spending too long haunted by the lives cut short, the devastated families, the permanently traumatised towns. I can make a clean-cut narrative out of the chaos. The victim's slain, the bad guy's caught and goes to jail, everyone moves on.

But there is one case that's been in my head lately, to say the least. I mean, I don't want to make this all about me, you understand—not yet, anyway. The true crime writer shouldn't *become* their own story—not unless they die, of course. But this one has got under my skin and I need to tell you why. If you're reading this, chances are it's already too late for me.

I learned about it by chance years ago, through hearing a talk on it at my local library and subsequently through reading snippets of my old hometown paper. I come a tiny town of a few thousand called New Mortby. You haven't heard of it? No, nor has anyone. Except those of us who were born there.

I'll try to put this together for you in a way that makes sense. It's mainly cobbled together from old articles, police reports, and the eyewitness testimony of a few people I interviewed. It's the only way you'll understand what's happening to me. It happened sixty-five years ago. Christmas Eve. A white Christmas, as it happened.

Now New Mortby was never known for a lot of things. But back then, one thing that *did* put it on the map was its Christmas decorations factory. People called it "the Christmas village" because kids would get broken decorations their parents brought home from the factory and hang them around their houses, even in the summer. So when the *actual* Christmas came round, it felt like the whole world was imitating little New Mortby for a few weeks.

That white Christmas sixty-five years ago, they must not have felt there was much to celebrate. The railway station had closed down three weeks before. That was New Mortby's only real link to the outside world. It's five miles from the next town over, a good twenty-five to the nearest city. Even in my childhood, buses didn't pass through all that often; it must've been even worse then. Those people must have felt like the whole world had abandoned them to their own devices.

The few people in New Mortby who didn't already work at the decorations factory had no choice after that. One of them was the guy who used to be the cleaner at the station, old Charlie Dockett.

Charlie was a loner. His folks died when he was young and, from what I can gather, he more or less brought himself up after that. The interviews in the aftermath of the tragedy all said more or less the same thing: "he kept to himself", "he didn't bother anyone", "he never said a word to me", "*you never would have guessed what he was planning*". But another thing true crime writing tells you is that these sorts of testimonies are always coloured by hindsight. If old Charlie Dockett had just been run over by a train—should such a thing have still been going through New Mortby—or dropped dead of a heart attack, the paper would have been full of glowing reviews. "Loner" would have become "unassuming, modest"—"gentle", even. "Old Charlie would've never harmed a soul."

The reports are unanimous in one thing: Charlie hated that factory. His supervisor was a bully boy who humiliated him in front of everyone more than once. He missed the freedom and fresh air his railway job had offered him, and on the few occasions he opened up to his colleagues he talked about it incessantly.

Christmas morning came. The snow arrived. And yet, not a single soul had left the factory after the night shift. This was strange; ironically, Christmas was a quiet time for the factory, since most places had already brought their stock for the year, so overtime was unlikely. They were making the baubles and tinsel for the *next* Christmas. Little did they know, Christmas in the real sense wouldn't come to New Mortby for a long time.

Early details were sketchy. The first newspaper report simply said: "TINSEL TERROR AT TOWN DECORATION FACTORY: MANY DEAD". Conflicting eyewitness statements described a rampage, a massacre, but didn't go into detail. Nobody could agree on what had happened exactly on that fateful Christmas Eve night.

One of the first police officers on the scene, Michael Stack, released a memoir about the case twenty years on. Of the eight emergency crew on the scene, he was the first and only one who ever dared to tell the story. All of those eight eventually left their jobs through stress, took on less demanding roles, or committed suicide. This case made ripples through so many lives.

As Stack tells it, as soon as the officers dropped by the factory, they knew something was very wrong.

They had to push open the doors of the place. And when they did, they were hit by that surprisingly sweet smell all officers come to know so intimately: the stench of bodies beginning to decompose. The machines had all got jammed and were beeping, not running anymore. The twelve people who were supposed to be manning them? All dead.

The bodies were placed back to back in the centre of the factory. They were all wearing party hats, dead eyes staring straight ahead. Someone had put paper plates in front of them and placed decorations on them, arranged as if they were food. One or two of them even had crackers stuffed into their dead hands. It looked like they were at a macabre Christmas party.

Every one of them had been strangled with tinsel.

They found Charlie Dockett not far away, hanging from a few bits of tinsel strung together to make them strong as rope. He was wearing a Santa hat. His face was locked in a horrified glare, as if he'd been scared to death. The flies were already buzzing around all of the bodies. Perhaps, after years of being lonely, old Charlie had finally got to be around people for Christmas.

It was a grim festive period after that. It made the national papers but, at that time of year, nobody wanted to dwell on it. A few well-wishers sent money to the grieving families. The town was inundated with sympathy cards. But the police and the townsfolk seemed most eager to forget all about old Charlie Dockett and his little Christmas massacre.

By the time I was born, Charlie Dockett and his victims lived on in only three ways. There were the skipping rope rhymes that mentioned him *"coming to kill you, whether you're naughty or nice"* and warned listeners to *"listen out for him in December—you'll hear him hanging in the wind"*. Nice, eh? There was the ramshackle building, long since burnt out and left to rack and ruin, that locals referred to casually as "the old factory". And there was a group of local history buffs who ran the "Justice for Dockett" group that gave badly attended talks at the local library. It was one of those that led me to the case in the first place, years ago. The woman giving the talk asked a series of questions: why would Charlie do such a thing—what was the motive? Was there any physical evidence against him, or was it just that he was hanging away from the others? And—most chillingly to my mind—how was he able to kill twelve able-bodied people, with seemingly very little struggle?

To that last one, there has never been a real answer.

For years, I've been able to put the so-called Tinsel Murders to the back of my mind. But not this year. Because I've been hearing some strange things. *Seeing* some strange things.

First off, I don't know where this tinsel came from. I find it in my living room every morning and I throw it away. But the next morning, I come downstairs and it's back. The red shine on it? I think that's blood. Nobody can get in or out of this house. No-one knows I'm staying here to write my new book. So who the hell keeps leaving it there?

And every night for the past two weeks, I've heard a swinging, creaking noise outside. I keep telling myself I'm imagining it. But when I looked outside last night, I swear I saw a figure hanging from my own garden tree. I ran down to see what it was and by the time I got there, there was nothing.

I'm not going to run from a ghost. But something tells me I won't be making it past Christmas. So just in case something happens, here's my story. Because if I'm going to go out, I want to be part of a true crime story—even a supernatural one. It's the only fair payback. And if it's my time, I don't want to go out in some dull, easily forgotten "the husband/wife did it" scenario. If you read this, I was killed by a ghost from Christmases long past. Pass it on.

In Santa's Grotto

You know the "Santas" who help out in shops, restaurants and town Christmas markets? Be careful around them.

Most are harmless, of course. 99% of them are just some nice guy trying to make a bit of extra cash for his family over the festive season. They're just a bloke in a fake white beard and a cheap red suit. But since we had one of the *other kind* come to our town, I've been freaked out by them all.

We had a Santa's Grotto open up on the outskirts of town that fateful year. No-one knew where it came from: that should have been the first clue something was strange about it. And they didn't charge to see Santa. *That* should have been a big, flashing neon sign saying "BEWARE!". Who pays for a Santa, all the decorations and a full-blown winter wonderland grotto without trying to cash in, at least a little bit?

But it was Christmas. Everyone's guard is down at Christmas. And the Grotto looked *so* Christmassy.

The kids flocked to the Grotto in their hundreds. It seemed such an innocent activity. A lot of parents let their children visit unaccompanied or with only an older sibling or cousin for company. That's what my small town was like: trusting. Slightly naïve, even. At least until the Christmas when Santa's Grotto came.

That first night, there was little sign of anything wrong. True, most kids came out with a faraway stare in their eyes. A lot of them refused to say anything about it, even whether they'd had a good time or not. A few came out with cheeks smeared with tears, saying they didn't like Santa anymore. But they were kids, right? Lots of kids are scared of Father Christmas. Nobody paid them much attention.

The next night, there were strange reports. I heard around town that the presents the Grotto was giving out to the kids were rotten. Some parents noticed a disgusting smell coming out of their children's wrapped boxes. When they opened them—much to the screaming indignation of the children whose gifts they were—they found rotten lumps of cheese. Vinegar-soaked rags. One mother found a dead rat in her boy's present.

A local senior police officer knew something was wrong when his crying granddaughter came back from the Grotto holding her present at arm's length.

"Santa's not friendly, Grandpa," she sobbed. "And the present he gave me is making scratchy sounds!"

The officer opened it carefully. Fat, juicy cockroaches burst out of it. Dozens of them. He dropped the box and stumbled backwards, the room ringing with his granddaughter's frenzied screams. The bugs scuttled into the dark corners of the house.

Five minutes after the police officer's granddaughter was traumatised, the first report of a child going missing at the Grotto was phoned in. Ten minutes after that, a second, separate report came. A boy and a girl. Five and eight years old, respectively.

It wasn't long until cop cars had the place surrounded. They cleared the remaining kids away and sent them home.

The first two officers burst in. As soon as their torches hit the creature that had been posing as Santa, it hissed and drew back. But they got enough of a look at it to see its huge insect eyes, its reptilian skin. The remains of its Santa disguise still hung off it—tufts of the beard still stuck to its scales; remnants of the red suit scattered on the ground. It seemed mid-transformation into its real form. The first officer took a step towards it. The creature reeled back, its twelve-inch long fangs still gnawing on the stripped-down leg bone of one of its child victims.

The officers rushed towards the now barely humanoid thing. It hissed and spat at them, then turned away. Just before they made contact with it, it threw itself down with incredible strength, hitting the ground face first. And its arms—now clearly belonging to a giant insect of some kind—began to burrow. It moved with superhuman speed. The officers were temporarily blinded by the dirt it threw up as it burrowed its way to escape.

By the time they reached the hole, it was already so deep they could barely see its retreating back, and the tunnel it had made was collapsing in behind it. The killer had escaped into the Earth.

The truth never came out, of course. In small towns it rarely does. Reputation is everything here; people close ranks. I think the families of the two victims, whose bones were found clean eaten away, might have been paid for their silence. They both moved away to start new lives in the next couple of years. I mean, wouldn't you?

Christmas has been muted here since then. There are a few decorations up, of course. Sometimes you hear people singing carols. But people shut their doors early here and hunker down behind lock and key, safe—especially in December. I've never seen Santa here since. Not even someone out on the town dressed as him or a kid's picture in a window.

So by all means, enjoy your kid's visit to Santa this year. I don't want to ruin your fun. But I beg you: look into the guy's eyes. Do you see something slightly shifty? Something... a bit reptilian? Are his movements a bit insectoid? Just be careful. That thing is still underground somewhere. The speed it moved, it could be anywhere in the world within a few days. And the Santa costume won it two meals in one night, once. Who knows when it'll pull the same trick again?

The Winter Plague

Being a gravedigger is harder in the winter. The frost makes the ground harder. You have to put all your strength into that first shovel break, as if you're digging into rock. The diggers in our village got a lot of practice.

I'd watch them from my garden at the crack of dawn. One man would shift the snow from the night before. Another would start the long process of digging that day's graves. When the plague began, it would only be one or two a week. The vicar would be there most mornings, muttering prayers over the dead, comforting their weeping families.

As the death toll increased, the funerals became increasingly hasty, and numerous. The vicar spent most of his days praying in the churchyard. Soon, there were too many deaths for single funerals to be practical. Mass graves became the norm. I wondered how they would fit any more around our small village's church. Having served as a place of rest for generations of our families, now it was full to bursting.

I've never been a good sleeper. Having been spared the deathly plague thus far, I put my insomnia to good use. I prayed. Ceaselessly. For an end to this horrible disease, which robbed people of their sight and hearing first, then gradually their movement, eventually leaving them as statues, quite devoid of any life. It wasn't just death, which comes for us all. It was the agonies that led to it. I sometimes wished I'd never been born than to witness even a single death from it, long, drawn-out, and without respite for their sufferings.

Some nights, in the silence in between prayers, I swore I could hear groaning in the full churchyard. This made me pray harder. If demons had brought this horrible fate to the village, I wasn't going to invite them in by looking out into the night to see them roaming around, looking for victims to devour.

The weather was continuously terrible. Our every escape was cut off by snow, which didn't seem to abate. Food and supplies were running low, but with fewer and fewer people around to use them up, starving was the least of our worries.

When the vicar himself succumbed to the illness, I wondered if God, too, had abandoned us. But still I prayed, trying my best to block out those ungodly groans. "Please, Lord, remove the unclean spirits. Give us rest. And deliver us from these horrors."

This morning, for the first time, I felt my prayers may have had some effect. The snows cleared enough to allow a single carriage through. Those few of us still surviving crowded around hungrily, hoping this stranger had brought some food and supplies. Maybe God had finally heard our pleas for help!

A well-dressed man got out of the carriage. I'd rarely seen his like around here. In the city maybe, clustered with other educated folk outside the universities, discussing astronomy and biology and new political ideas from the continent.

Those of us closest to him immediately fired questions his way, but he silenced us by holding up an open hand.

He blinked furiously as his eyes swept across the expanse of our village. They came to rest on the churchyard, its grounds cut up from the dozens of recent burials, and widened in horror.

He pointed a shaking finger at the churchyard.

"How many are buried here?"

"Too many, sir," I replied. "The sickness has taken most of our village."

"Gather the gravediggers immediately!" he shouted. His sudden outburst made many of us gasp. "Any able-bodied man, woman, or child—dig up as many as you can, starting with the most recently buried! Use whatever tools you have to hand. God damn it all, do it *quickly*!"

Us survivors muttered among ourselves.

"But sir," I spoke up again, aghast, "we can't disturb the peace of the dead! It's a terrible sacrilege—"

The man looked straight at me. I noticed all the blood had drained from his cheeks.

"*They're not dead!* The disease doesn't kill its unfortunate victims. It incapacitates them, yes. Induces in them a death-like stupor—yes! But after a day, two at most, they slowly regain their faculties!"

His words washed over me like a sudden storm. I felt as if I would pass out or die of horror at the consequences of his words.

Despite the weakness brought on by our starvation, every survivor sprang into action. We grabbed spades, broke doors to use as makeshift diggers, and even scooped up the earth with our hands. Our fingers were torn, bloodied and without fingernails by the time we unearthed the first victims of the plague.

The vicar was the first one we unburied. He was one of the few we'd afforded a coffin, since the idea of throwing him into the mass graves felt almost sacrilegious. One of the gravediggers shoved the end of a spade into the gap between the coffin's body and its lid. With a groan of effort, he pushed it down, breaking it in two and exposing our poor, dear clergyman to the elements.

The first thing that hit us was the stench. I gagged on the smell of death. As it cleared, we move forwards. His face was shrivelled and discoloured, his skin falling away, his cadaveric features warped by decay. But his eyes were open. His face was set in a horrifying silent scream. And his hands were torn and stained with blood, like ours. The broken lid of his casket was covered with dents and desperate scratches.

Without a word, we moved to the next victims. Everyone we dug up had that same ungodly expression, like they'd died viewing hell itself. The ones in the mass graves had mud in their mouths, their faces bloated from lack of air as they'd tried desperately to breathe—and felt nothing but mud against their faces.

We worked until the sun began to set.

I swear I heard demonic laughter on the wind. I tried to pray to God but the words didn't come. None of us met each other's eyes as we dug, longing for a miracle, a single survivor—and all in vain. How could any of us hope for salvation after this?

Haunted by Christmas Past

For Ricky, Christmas had always been about the food. Even as a kid, presents were secondary.

He still sent Santa a list as long as his arm—what kid didn't?—but it was the Christmas Day meal that was the highlight of the year. Grandparents, aunts and uncles around, cousins to play with, crackers, turkey and chocolatey dessert. Mmm. What could ever be better than that?

Tucking into his meal last Christmas, he felt that joyous contentment of his childhood Christmases wash over him again. The difficulties and tedium of adult life melted gently off him like snow in the sunshine.

The room was set up perfectly: decorated beautifully with a gorgeous, flowery centrepiece. Tinsel and fairy lights hung over every wall. The tree was in the corner, so tall its tip touched the ceiling. He could hear the laughter of the family around him. He let some of the turkey melt in his mouth and washed it down with a fine wine.

Letting out a quiet sigh, he turned to his left. Trisha looked beautiful today—more so than usual, even. He reached across to his girlfriend and took her hand in his.

"I think this might be the best one yet," he whispered. She grinned.

"This is glorious, Ricky," she said. "I wish it could last forever."

For a moment, anything seemed possible. He imagined future Christmas Days with their own children running around their legs:

in his mind's eye, they had his green eyes and Trisha's flowing blonde hair. Cherubic mixtures of their own best features.

There was a buzzing sound, and suddenly everything came to a crashing halt.

Ricky's VR headset was pulled unceremoniously off his head, catching a couple of hairs from his temple and sending a shock of pain through his face.

Just like that, he was back in the warehouse. The twinkling, magical fairy lights were replaced with the harsh strobes overhead. His supervisor, a burly creature called Eddie, glared into his face, still holding his headset.

"Time's up! Back to work!" he barked. Ricky had worked under Eddie for eight years and had still not had even a passing pleasantry from him.

Ricky stood up, struggling to shake off the feelings the Christmas simulation had stirred up. His shift was still only halfway through; he needed to get back in the game if he wanted to meet his item picking targets for today and be allowed to go to the sleeping pods on time tonight.

Trisha rubbed her eyes, standing up next to him. He looked at her: those dark bags were back under her eyes and she had that pale complexion again. He felt a mixture of sympathy and frustration. If they completed six 12-hour shifts of picking in a week, workers dating pickers from other departments were allowed a ten minute video call together. Trisha had been periodically passing out on duty for the past couple of weeks and had missed both of their last scheduled times as a punishment. She'd used up all her medical attention credits on the broken ankle she'd picked up a year before. By the looks of her, Ricky thought, they wouldn't make this week's call either.

The half hour Christmas break seemed to go quicker every year. But at least this year they'd been scheduled for the same slot.

Trisha's supervisor took her by the shoulders and led her to the little buggy that was going to take workers from her division back to their stations for the rest of their shifts. Ricky's eyes stuck wordlessly on hers.

Behind him, he could hear Eddie screaming at him to hurry up and run back to his station, or else. But his threats seemed to blur into the background just this once.

He watched Trisha's cohort drive away. If they were lucky, they would get assigned to the same slot for the summer party VR simulation next July. Neither of them broke their gaze as she got further and further down the impossibly long warehouse corridor.

About the Author

Charlotte O'Farrell has loved horror for as long as she can remember. With her writing, she wants to share that love with her readers.

She writes short stories and novellas. Her stories have appeared in dozens of anthologies from a variety of independent publishers, covering every sub-genre of horror around. She writes about all manner of the creepy, weird and wonderful.

Charlotte lives in Nottingham, UK with her husband, daughter and the obligatory black cat.

MORE CHILLS FROM VELOX BOOKS

SPIRALING DOWN
DISTURBING HORROR STORIES BY
MICHAEL MARKS

PLASTIC FACES
UNSETTLING STORIES BY
MARTA ABROMAITYTE

THESE LONELY PLACES

I'VE DONE THIS BEFORE
A BARRAGE OF NIGHTMARES BY RYAN MAJOR

VERY DARK THOUGHTS
A COLLECTION OF TERRIFYING TALES
KYLE HARRISON

IRON MAIDENS
TWISTED TALES OF KILLER WOMEN
SARAH JANE HUNTINGTON

STRANGE TALES OF THE MACABRE
TALES BY E. REYES

FACE DOWN IN THE GRAVE
SINISTER TALES BY
THOMAS O.

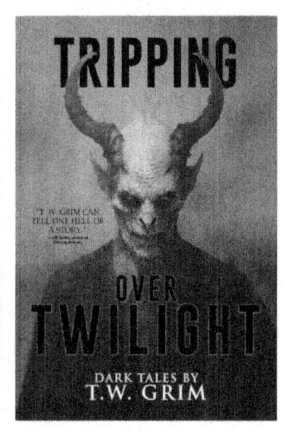

TRIPPING OVER TWILIGHT
DARK TALES BY
T.W. GRIM

MORE CHILLS FROM VELOX BOOKS

UNCLEAN SPIRITS
HORRIFYING STORIES BY BIKRAM MANN

HOUSE WITH ONE HUNDRED DOORS
AND OTHER DARK TALES BY TRAVIS BROWN

ONE EYE OPEN
STRANGE STORIES FOR PECULIAR PEOPLE — K.G. LEWIS

FROM THE DEPTHS
TERRIFYING TALES BY RICHARD SAXON

NO MORE FUEL
100% UNFILTERED
TALES OF HORROR BY TOM RUSSELL

THE MOONLIT ROAD
A MUST FOR LOVERS OF HORROR
SHORT HORROR STORIES BY WILLIAM STUART

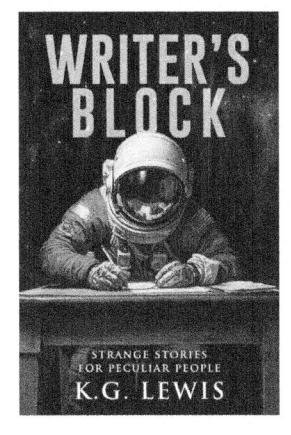

WRITER'S BLOCK
STRANGE STORIES FOR PECULIAR PEOPLE
K.G. LEWIS

YOUR WORST FEARS
A DECK OF DISTURBING TALES BY HANNAH COSTIN

FRIGHT BITES
SHORT TALES OF TERROR BY MICAH EDWARDS

MORE CHILLS FROM VELOX BOOKS

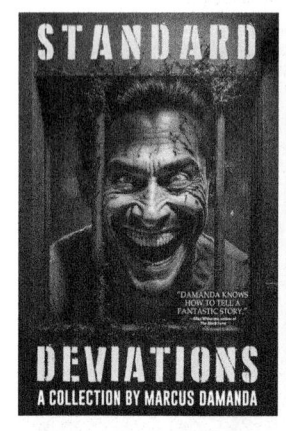

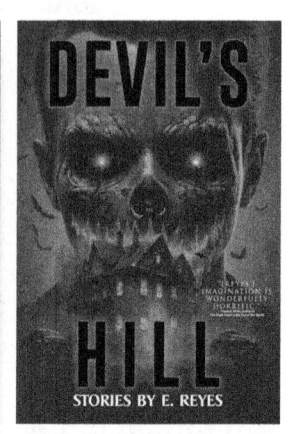

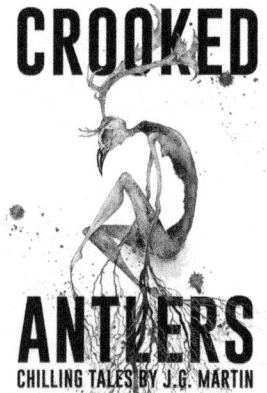

STANDARD DEVIATIONS
A COLLECTION BY MARCUS DAMANDA

AFTER TASTE
AND OTHER STORIES BY BRETT O'REILLY

DEVIL'S HILL
STORIES BY E. REYES

WE WILL FIND A PLACE FOR YOU
A COLLECTION OF HORROR BY ELFORD ALLEY
Foreword by T.L. Bodine

THE THINGS THEY TAKE AWAY
CHILLING TALES BY T.J. LEA

IF HELL IS WHAT YOU WANT
THE COLLECTED SHORT FICTION OF RAFAEL MARMOL

SIZING UP YOUR SHADOW
DARK TALES BY MATT RICHARDSEN

HEAD GAMES
STRANGE STORIES FOR PECULIAR PEOPLE
K.G. LEWIS

CROOKED ANTLERS
CHILLING TALES BY J.C. MARTIN

Printed in Great Britain
by Amazon